Written by Tim Kennington
Illustrated by Josy Bloggs and Liz Kay
Cover illustration by Josy Bloggs
Edited by Gary Panton
Designed by Jack Clucas
Cover design by John Bigwood

union
square
kids

NEW YORK

UNION SQUARE KIDS and the distinctive Union Square Kids logo are trademarks of Union Square & Co., Inc.

Union Square & Co., LLC, is a subsidiary of Sterling Publishing Co., Inc.

First published in Great Britain in 2021 by Buster Books, an imprint of
Michael O'Mara Books Limited 9 Lion Yard, Tremadoc Road, London SW4 7NQ, England

First Union Square Kids edition published in 2023.
ISBN 978-1-4549-4759-2

Library of Congress Cataloging-in-Publication Data

Names: Kennington, Tim author. | Bloggs, Josy, illustrator. | Kay, Liz,
    illustrator.
Title: This book is full of brains : all kinds of brains and how they work
    / written by Tim Kennington ; illustrated by Josy Bloggs, and Liz Kay.
Other titles: All kinds of brains and how they work
Description: First Union Square Kids edition. | New York : Union Square
    Kids [2023] | Includes index. | Audience: Ages 8-12 | Audience: Grades
    4-6 | Summary: "Did you know that a fully grown human brain is equal to
    the weight of one 12-week-old kitten? Or that it can think at 4 1/2
    times the speed of a cheetah? How about the fact that an octopus brain
    reaches to the tips of its tentacles, or that the emerald jewel wasp can
    use mind control over other insects? Filled with interesting facts,
    immersive at-home activities, and fun optical illusions, This Book Is
    Full of Brains will make kids fall in love with all types of
    brains-whether they be human, dinosaur, or robot!"-- Provided by
    publisher.
Identifiers: LCCN 2022024743 | ISBN 9781454947592 (hardcover)
Subjects: LCSH: Brain--Juvenile literature. | Brain--Physiology--Juvenile
    literature. | Thought and thinking--Juvenile literature.
Classification: LCC QP376 .K56 2023 | DDC 612.8/2--dc23/eng/20220525
LC record available at https://lccn.loc.gov/2022024743

For information about custom editions, special sales, and premium purchases,
please contact specialsales@unionsquareandco.com.

Manufactured in China

Lot #:
2   4   6   8   10   9   7   5   3   1
02/23

unionsquareandco.com

THIS
BOOK IS
FULL OF
BRAINS

union
square
kids

NEW YORK

CONTENTS

Any time you see this icon, it means there's something for you to try yourself at home.

CONGRATULATIONS!

You are the proud owner of something incredible . . . a brain!
You probably haven't even noticed it, but your brain is constantly
helping you to understand everything that is around you.

It's not just humans who have incredible brains, either. In the
pages that follow, you'll find out about animal brains, dinosaur
brains, and even robot brains.

Because brains are so amazing, lots of scientists study them
and try to understand exactly how they work. These scientists
are called neuroscientists. By reading this book, you're making
your first steps to becoming a neuroscientist too.

It's time to **BLOW** your mind!

If you come across any words you don't know,
don't worry. Check out the Glossary on page 92,
where some of the harder words are explained.

1

BRAIN BASICS

Your brain is super-powered! It makes one quintillion calculations every second. That's a bigger number than the number of stars in our galaxy. If you had one quintillion grains of rice, they would fill the Empire State Building 85,000 times over!

In fact, some scientists believe your brain is more powerful than every computer in the world put together.

But what is your brain? What does it look like? How does it work? And how does it connect to the rest of your body?

It's time to meet your brilliant brain.

HOW BIG IS YOUR BRAIN?

IT'S NOT BIG, BUT IT IS CLEVER

Unless you're able to take a look inside your head, you'll never see how big your brain is. So how do you find out about its size, shape and how much it weighs?

 **TRY IT AT HOME: MAKE A FIST OF IT**

Luckily, there is a very easy way to find out your brain's size. Ball both hands into fists and hold them together. Your two fists are about the same size as your brain.

Your fists show the rough shape of your brain too. Its ridges and folds are a bit like the bumps and grooves of your knuckles and fingers.

WEIGHT WATCHING

A fully grown brain weighs about 2.8 lbs (1.3 kg). That's roughly the same as 11 bananas or:

- One 12-week-old kitten
- Two squirrels
- 1,350 chocolate chips

EINSTEIN'S MARVELOUS MIND

Not every brain is the same size or shape. Take the brain of Albert Einstein, for example. He was one of the cleverest scientists who ever lived. That would make his brain bigger and heavier than everyone else's, right?

WRONG!

When Einstein died in 1955, scientists discovered that his brain was actually lighter than most other people's. However, Einstein's *parietal lobe* was 15% bigger than the average. This makes sense because the parietal lobe is the part of the brain that handles math and sums, and math was Einstein's thing!

$$E = mc^2$$

Albert Einstein ——

DID YOU KNOW?
Your brain might look tough like an old pink raisin, but it's actually very soft, wet, and wobbly.

In fact, three-quarters of your brain is just water, so you could think of it as being like an incredibly clever piece of gelatin.

YOUR BRAIN'S LIFE STORY

HOW YOUR BRAIN GROWS (AND SHRINKS)

Your brain grows as you grow, but did you know that it eventually starts to shrink? Here's a look at how the size of your brain changes throughout your life.

FETUS

The first sign of your brain appeared after just 25 days. At this stage, your whole body was roughly the size of a poppy seed! Something called a *neural tube* appeared, which later became your brain and spinal cord.

BABY

Three months after your birth, your brain was double the size it was when you were born. At this point your brain was the size of an apple and half the size of an adult brain.

CHILD

In the first few years of life, you had to learn how everything in the world works, as well as how to walk and talk. A toddler's brain is 80% of the size of an adult's brain, but twice as busy!

ADULT

You might have done most of your growing by the time you reach 18, but that doesn't mean you will have a grown-up brain. The parts of your brain that help you make sensible decisions and spot danger will keep developing until you're around 25 years old.

OLD AGE

By the age of 40, your brain will become less active. It will actually start shrinking and lose about 5% of its size every ten years. By the time you reach 60 or 70, the parts of your brain controlling memory will begin to be affected.

PROTECTING YOUR BRAIN
WHY A SKULL IS NOT DULL

Your brain is fragile and needs your bony skull to protect
it from accidents. But it takes more than just a skull to
cushion your brain from the dangers of everyday life.

TRY IT AT HOME:
THE JAR EGGS-PERIMENT

Find an egg. It's going to represent your brain. If you put the egg in a jar, the egg is protected by the glass, just like your brain is protected by your skull. But what happens if you shake the jar? **OOPS!** It's bye-bye egg.

Instead, try filling the jar with water. Screw on the lid and give the jar a shake.

The water protects the egg from being bashed against the sides of the jar. Inside your skull, your brain is surrounded by a layer of liquid called *cerebrospinal fluid (CSF)*. CSF stops your brain from hitting the inside of your skull—just as the water protects that egg.

SOFT SPOTS

Your skull isn't just one big bone. It's made of 22 different bones that have fused together. However, when you were first born, these bones hadn't quite joined up yet.

On a newborn baby's head there are two places called *fontanelles*—or soft spots—where there are still gaps in the skull. Most babies' fontanelles close up after a few months.

Hyoid bone

Tongue

WHY DON'T WOODPECKERS GET SORE BRAINS?

Have you ever seen a woodpecker tapping on a tree? They're able to move their heads back and forth 20 times a second!

You might think a woodpecker would need an extra-hard skull to cope with all that pecking, but in reality it has a soft, spongy skull that acts like a cushion. A bone called the *hyoid bone* acts just like a seat belt, holding the brain in place.

The weirdest part, though, is the woodpecker's tongue. It's so long that it wraps all the way around the top of the bird's brain!

FEELING NERVOUS

WHAT IS THE NERVOUS SYSTEM?

You might think your brain just floats about in your head, zapping out instructions, but it's a lot more complex than that. The brain works together with other parts of your body to form the nervous system.

This diagram shows the main parts of your nervous system.

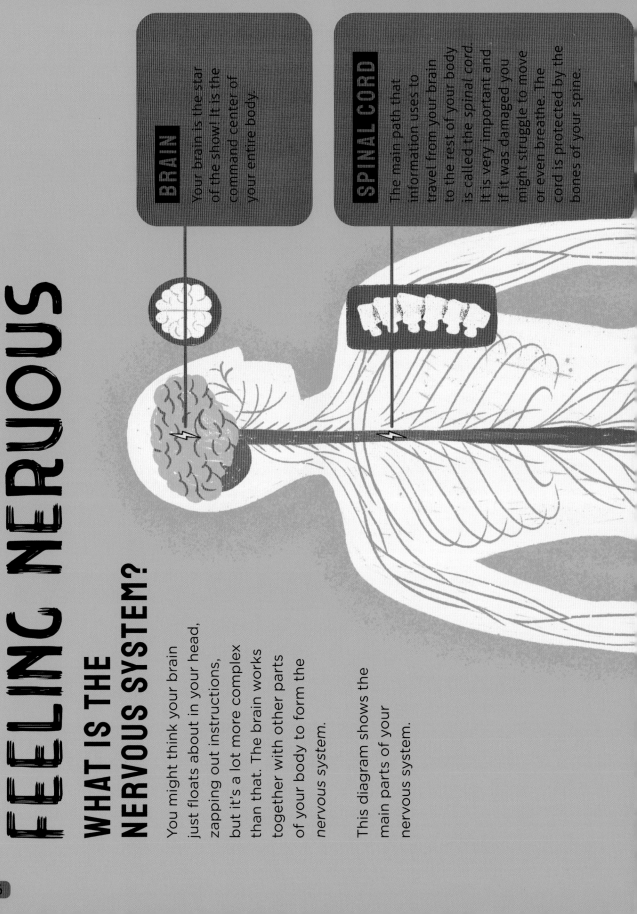

BRAIN

Your brain is the star of the show! It is the command center of your entire body.

SPINAL CORD

The main path that information uses to travel from your brain to the rest of your body is called the *spinal cord*. It is very important and if it was damaged you might struggle to move or even breathe. The cord is protected by the bones of your spine.

NERVES

Nerves run all through your body, sending your brain's commands to the different parts. You have around 38 miles (60 kilometers) of nerves in your body.

DID YOU KNOW?

Not every part of your body has nerves running through it. Your hair, for example, only has nerves at the bottom (the root). That's why it hurts if somebody pulls your hair out, but not when you have a haircut.

ALL SYSTEMS GO

The nervous system is the most important system in your whole body. It controls all these different functions:

Intelligence, learning, memory, and all your thoughts and feelings

 Movement, so that you can dance, run, draw, and smile

 Basic body functions that you don't even think about, such as breathing, digesting, sweating, and shivering

 Senses (that's sight, hearing, taste, touch, and smell)

Your ability to notice and react to pain

2

INSIDE THE BRAIN

Imagine you were building a school and you decided to put everything in one giant room. Science lessons would happen in the place where you ate your lunch, which would also be the same room as the toilets. It would be pretty hard to concentrate with so much going on in the same place, right?

Your brain also needs different "rooms" to work at its best. It is split into sections that do different things. This means it can do lots of jobs at once, without getting confused. That's why you can read this book, breathe, and blink all at the same time (oh, and your heart keeps beating, too).

This chapter explores each of the brain's "rooms" to find out what they do.

BRAIN MAP
TAKE A TOUR OF YOUR BRAIN

A brain might look like one pink blob, but it's divided into sections that each have their own jobs. This diagram shows the main sections of a human brain.

CEREBELLUM

The *cerebellum* is your body's steering wheel. It controls some body movements, as well as your ability to balance.

BRAINSTEM

The *brainstem* controls a lot of things your body does without you noticing, such as breathing, swallowing food, and sleeping.

CEREBRUM

The *cerebrum* controls your personality and preferences. If you love to bungee-jump, that's due to your cerebrum. You could say it's the part that makes you who you are.

DID YOU KNOW?

The cerebrum is made up of two halves, known as the right and left *hemispheres*. These perform different jobs and focus on different things. Weirdly, the right hemisphere controls the movement of the left side of your body, and the left hemisphere controls the movement of the right side of your body.

THE CEREBELLUM

A LITTLE BRAIN CONTROLLING LITTLE MOVEMENTS

You know when you hear your favorite music and can't help but dance around? It's your *cerebellum* that is making your toes tap and your buttocks wiggle. It takes information from your senses, your spinal cord, and other bits of your brain, and uses it to control your movements.

This is a diagram of a human brain with the cerebellum area enlarged to show its main parts.

POSTERIOR LOBE

The *posterior lobe* controls your *fine motor skills*. Your fine motor skills include your ability to pick things up, play video games, write with a pen, and do all the other things for which you need your hands and fingers.

ANTERIOR LOBE

The *anterior lobe* controls the little movements your body makes that you don't even think about. That's everything from tiny muscle twitches to flinching if something gets thrown at you.

FLOCCULONODULAR LOBE

The *flocculonodular lobe* (pronounced "flock-yoo-loe-nod-you-lur") looks after your sense of balance. It comes in handy if you don't want to fall over!

TRY IT AT HOME: THE BALANCE TEST

You can check your flocculonodular lobe is working by testing your balance. Stand up straight and slowly lean forward. Eventually, you'll start to wobble. That's because your center of gravity (which was just above your belly button when you were standing straight) is no longer directly above your feet. This sends a message to your brain, which then makes you wobble to try to keep you from falling over.

THE BRAINSTEM
KEEPING YOUR BODY GOING

Your *brainstem* controls lots of things that you often don't even notice. It tells your heart to beat, your lungs to breathe, and many other things besides. Here are the main parts of the brainstem and what they do.

MIDBRAIN

The *midbrain* takes everything you see and hear and processes it so the rest of your brain can understand it.

TRY IT AT HOME: TEST YOUR MIDBRAIN

Focus on an object in front of you and keep looking at it while moving your head. The object should stay in the same place, even though your head is moving around. That's because your midbrain is making sure that what you look at remains stable.

PONS

Although you can choose to hold your breath, breathing mainly happens without you having to think about it. That is controlled by the *pons*.

The pons also plays a part in how you sleep and helps you understand what you are tasting. Next time you enjoy a bowl of spaghetti bolognese or a slice of cake, you'll know your pons is doing its job.

MEDULLA

No matter how hard you try, you can't tell your heart not to beat. That's because of your *medulla*, which controls how blood and oxygen travel through your body.

Your heartbeat is an *involuntary action*. In other words, it's something your body does that you can't control.

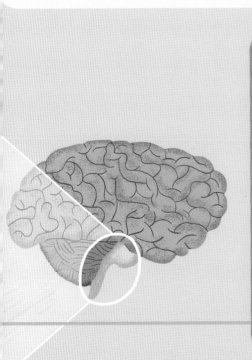

COULD YOU SURVIVE WITH JUST A BRAINSTEM?

Could you survive if the brainstem was the only working brain part that you had? Technically, yes. You would still be able to breathe and swallow, and your heart would still pump blood around your body.

However, you would not be able to think or understand anything that was happening around you. It would probably be very scary, except for the fact that the part of your brain that processes fear wouldn't be working!

THE CEREBRUM
MAKING YOU WHO YOU ARE

The *cerebrum* is the largest part of your brain. It controls your voluntary actions, as well as your hearing and vision. It even defines your emotions and personality. This diagram shows the four main parts of the cerebrum.

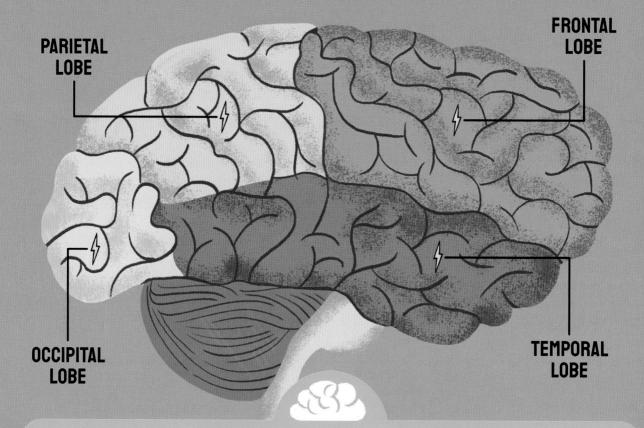

PARIETAL LOBE

FRONTAL LOBE

OCCIPITAL LOBE

TEMPORAL LOBE

DID YOU KNOW?

The lumps and bumps that cover your brain are called *gyri*. Gyri give the brain a larger area, which means it has more space to do its work. Only larger mammals have gyri. A rat's brain, for example, is completely smooth.

The gyri also separate your brain's different parts, which stops you from getting very confused.

Gyri

No gyri

FRONTAL LOBE

The *frontal lobe* controls the key areas that define your personality and ability to communicate.
Find out more on pages 28–29.

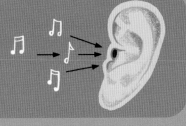

PARIETAL LOBE

The *parietal lobe* processes information from your nerves, so you can understand if you're touching something soft like a furry pet or hot like a boiling pan.
Find out more on pages 30–31.

TEMPORAL LOBE

The *temporal lobe* turns the vibrations of your eardrums into sounds that you can understand.
Find out more on pages 32–33.

OCCIPITAL LOBE

The *occipital lobe* enables you to understand everything your eyes see.
Find out more on pages 34–35.

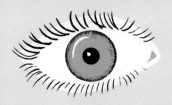

VOLUNTARY OR INVOLUNTARY ACTIONS?

Voluntary actions are the movements you actively think about. They could be small, such as picking up a grain of rice, or big, like a triple flip on a trampoline.

Involuntary actions are the ones you don't think about, such as blinking and breathing.

THE FRONTAL LOBE

The frontal lobe is the front of your cerebrum. It is the bit that gives you your thoughts, ideas, and personality.

MOTOR CORTEX

The *motor cortex* controls voluntary movements, such as walking, running, dancing, and karate kicks.

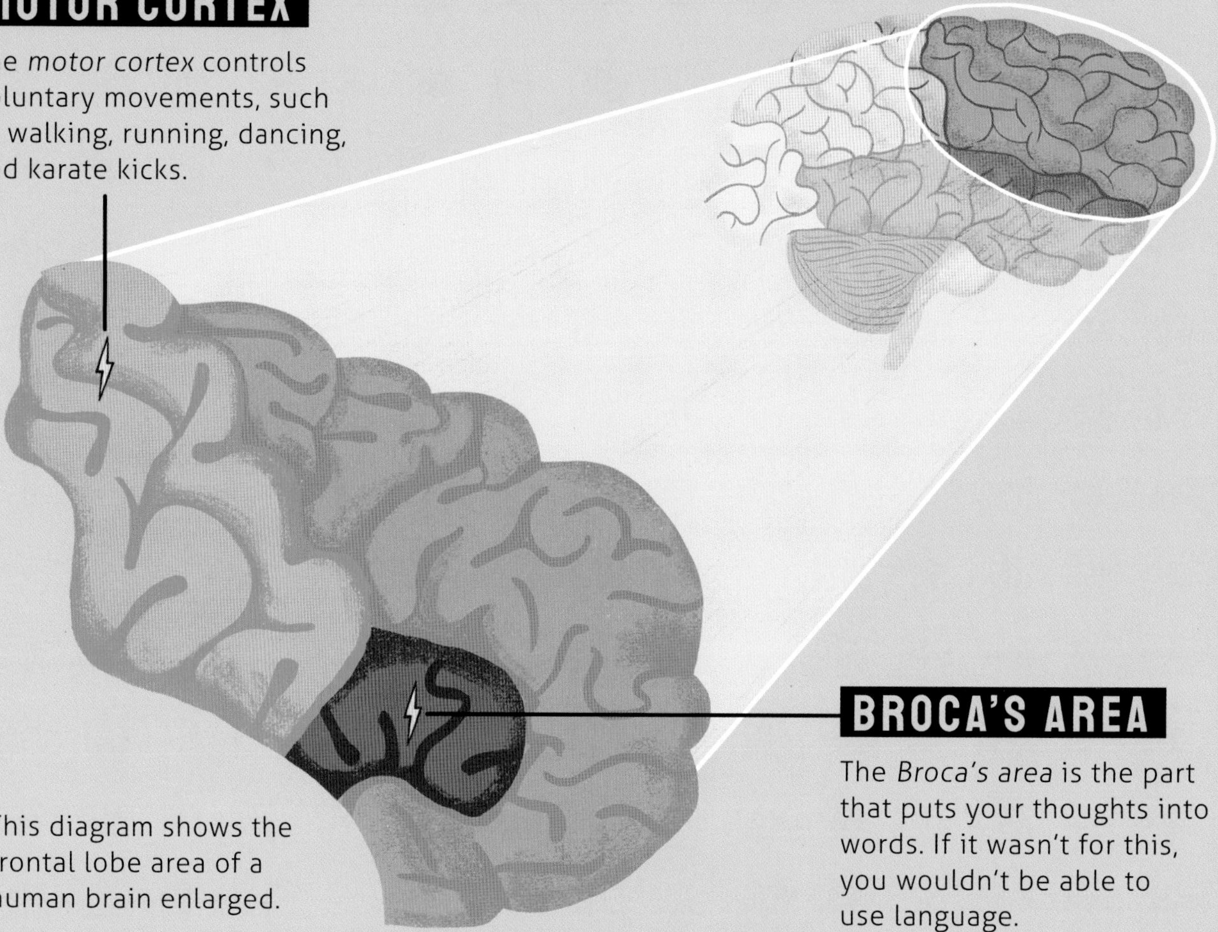

This diagram shows the frontal lobe area of a human brain enlarged.

BROCA'S AREA

The *Broca's area* is the part that puts your thoughts into words. If it wasn't for this, you wouldn't be able to use language.

WHAT MAKES YOU YOU?

The following things contribute to making you the person you are, and they're all controlled by the frontal lobe.

RECOGNITION
Knowing what things are and being able to tell them apart.

PERSONALITY
All the things you like and dislike, from the games you love to the songs you hate.

LONG-TERM MEMORY
The long-term memories you'll hopefully still have when you're old and grey. You might even remember reading this book.

EMPATHY
Your ability to care for other people because you understand how they feel. Empathy is why you feel sad when something bad happens to someone else, even though it didn't happen to you.

TRY IT AT HOME: TEST YOUR FRONTAL LOBE

The frontal lobe controls muscle movement as well as the ability to recognize patterns. You can easily put yours to the test, using something called the Luria test.

All you have to do is learn a pattern of three movements and then repeat them over and over as quickly as you can. Are you ready?

1. Hit the table with your fist (be gentle)

2. Hit the table with the palm of your hand

3. Hit the table with the side of your hand (karate chop)

Can you repeat the pattern three times without looking at the instructions?
CONGRATULATIONS! Your frontal lobe just passed the test.

THE PARIETAL LOBE

Every time you touch something, the parietal lobe
receives the message from millions of nerves in your skin.

Here's a diagram of the human
parietal lobe so you can have a
deeper look at this very useful
section of brain.

PARIETAL ASSOCIATION CORTEX

The *parietal association cortex* is
what you're using right now to look
at these words and understand what
they mean.

If it wasn't for this part of the brain,
you wouldn't be able to recognize
the shapes and symbols you know
better as numbers and letters.

PRIMARY SOMATOSENSORY CORTEX

The *primary somatosensory cortex*
processes your feelings of touch (so
that you know if something is hot,
sharp, or soft, for example). Without it,
you wouldn't be able to hold an object
without dropping it, sit down in a chair
without missing it, or even walk in a
straight line.

TRY IT AT HOME: TRICK OF THE MIND

Your parietal lobe can help you to tell the difference between something that looks small because it's far away, and something that is just plain small. But did you know that you can trick it?

Below is a Ponzo illusion, which is a visual trick that was first created over 100 years ago. It looks a little like a railway track going off into the distance, with a yellow line toward the bottom and another one near the top.

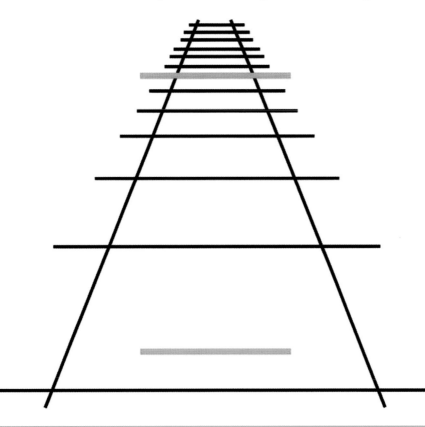

Which of the two yellow lines do you think is longer?

The yellow line at the top looks like it's longer, right? But they're actually both exactly the same length. You can even measure them to check. If you thought one was longer than the other, don't worry. It simply means your parietal lobe is working just the way it should.

THE TEMPORAL LOBE

The temporal lobe deals with hearing sounds and understanding language. It also stores some short-term memories, which comes in handy for understanding what's going on around you. Here's how it's divided up.

AMYGDALA

The *amygdala* is where your brain stores memories about emotions. It's how you know that a smiling person is happy and a frowning person is sad or worried.

AUDITORY CORTEX

The *auditory cortex* is dedicated to sounds and language. It helps you to recognize where a sound is coming from and what is making it. It also enables you to recognize the sounds that make up words.

HYPOTHALAMUS

The *hypothalamus* has a very important role—it lets you know if you get hungry or thirsty.

HIPPOCAMPUS

The *hippocampus* helps you to learn and remember facts. You can use tricks to help it recall things. For example, if you think you might struggle to remember the word "hippocampus," try thinking of some hippos in a tent. Hippo campers!

TRY IT AT HOME: MEMORY MAGIC

Storing a lot of information in your short-term memory can be difficult. Try studying this list of words for as long as you like. Then cover the words up, take a piece of paper, and see how many you can write down from memory. You'll probably find it's not as easy as it looks.

Potato

Cactus

Shower

Chimpanzee

Tuesday

Hot

Violin

Telephone

Happy

Spain

Professor

TOP TIP

To help memorize the things on the list, try thinking of them together in funny situations. For example, to remember the words happy, chimpanzee, cactus, and violin, you could imagine a happy chimpanzee sitting on a cactus while playing a violin. That's not an image you're likely to forget in a hurry.

THE OCCIPITAL LOBE

How do you tell the difference between a duck and a realistic statue of a duck? By using your occipital lobe! It's the part of your cerebrum that takes what your eyes are seeing and translates it into images you can make sense of. This diagram shows you where the occipital lobe is found in a human brain.

PRIMARY VISUAL CORTEX

The *primary visual cortex* takes all the light coming in through your eyes and turns it into pictures.

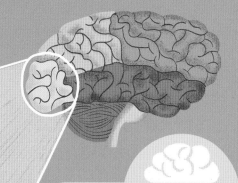

DID YOU KNOW?
While most of your memory is handled by other parts of your brain, it's important that your occipital lobe has some memory, too. If it didn't, you'd forget what you're looking at every time you blink!

DON'T I KNOW YOU?
Have you ever heard of a condition called "face blindness"? People who have it are unable to recognize faces, so even their friends and family look like strangers to them. That's because part of their occipital lobe isn't working properly. A healthy occipital lobe doesn't just allow you to see things—it allows you to recognize them, too.

JESS

OSCAR

TRY IT YOUSELF: TRICK OF THE MIND

Does the picture on this page look like it's moving? Don't panic—it's just an optical illusion. Your brain has to process everything your eyes see, but this combination of colors and shapes is giving your brain so much information that it creates some crazy effects. The wheels look like they're turning, but in actual fact nothing is moving at all. Very cool, right?

How good are you at putting a face to a name? Study these names and faces for one minute, then cover up their names and test yourself. Could you remember all their names?

ASIM

AMELIA

HARSHA

HOW YOU SEE WHAT YOU SEE
SIGHT'S INCREDIBLE JOURNEY

Everything your eyes look at has to travel all the way to the back of your brain. This diagram shows the pathway your sight follows to get from your eye to your brain.

I. FROM YOUR EYE

Your eye's job is simply to collect light. When you look at an object (like this toy duck), what you're actually seeing is the light bouncing off that object and traveling into your eyes.

SHRIMP SIGHT

Most humans can see three colors (red, blue, and green) from which all other colors are made. However, some animals have eyes that see the world very differently.

The mantis shrimp has the world's most complicated eyes. Its eyes have five times more sensors than human eyes, so can see types of light that people can't.

2. ALONG YOUR OPTIC NERVE

Your eyes have 120 million cells called *rods* (which pick up light, dark, and shapes) and six million cells called *cones* (which pick up colors). Together, they gather up all that information and send it along your *optic nerve* toward your brain.

3. TO YOUR BRAIN

After traveling along your optic nerve, the information reaches the *visual cortex* in the back of your brain, where it is processed into images you can understand, recognize, and remember.

TRY IT AT HOME: COLOR CHECK

People who are *color blind* don't see colors in the normal way. One way to test for this condition is with a picture called an *Ishihara plate*. Can you see a number in the circle below? Someone who is color blind might find it difficult to see.

An Ishihara plate

DID YOU KNOW?

Your eye's lens curves the light, which means that by the time it reaches your brain the image is upside down. You can actually recreate this at home by looking at something through a glass ball. Don't worry, though. Your brain knows to flip it around the right way.

⌂ IS SEEING BELIEVING?

You've already seen a few ways that your eyes can trick your brain into seeing things that are not really there. Here are a few more optical illusions for you to try out. Is your mind blown?

PARALLEL LINES?

Take a look at this tilting table. Is it really tilting?

Look below. Are the horizontal lines curved or straight?

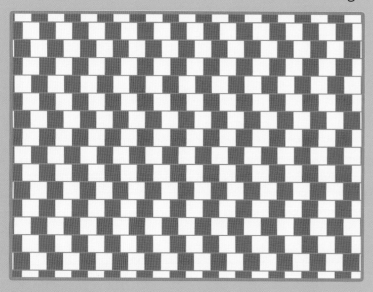

In both of these illusions, the horizontal lines are completely straight and parallel. However, the other lines and shapes trick your brain into thinking that they're not.

SHADES OF GRAY

Take a look at the checkered grid. Which of the two squares marked with an "X" do you think is darker?

How about this time? Which of the two gray columns is darker?

Both illusions actually only contain one shade of gray! They seem like different shades because your brain isn't able to look at just one thing. It takes information from the full surroundings and uses it to help you understand what is happening. If you cover up the surrounding colors in each illusion, you'll see that the shades are the same.

3

HOW YOU THINK

Did you know that you have over 6,000 thoughts every day? Each one of those thoughts sends tiny sparks of electricity whizzing through your brain and out to your body. But what is actually happening in your brain when you think?

Your brain is full of tiny messengers that all work together to make sure your thoughts and ideas get to the right place as quickly as possible. They create paths that link all the separate parts of your brain together, as well as connecting your brain to the rest of your nervous system.

It's time to find out all about the wonders of thought, and send a few more electric sparks sizzling through your brain.

ARE BRAINS ELECTRIC?

THE CIRCUIT IN YOUR BODY

Have you ever seen a picture of someone with a big light bulb drawn above their head to show that they've had a great idea? Your brain doesn't really have a light bulb, but it *is* electric.

Each command your brain sends out is a tiny electrical signal. Your nerves act like wires carrying those signals around your body. So your whole nervous system is just like an electric circuit.

BRAIN POWER!

Your brain can generate about 12–25 watts of electricity. That's enough to power an LED light bulb.

⚡

Every single movement you make happens because an electric command has been zapped out to your body.

⚡

When you sleep, your brain runs important tasks to help it perform better the next day. It's a bit like charging a cell phone overnight.

A MONSTROUS TALE

In a story written by Mary Shelley in 1818, a doctor called Frankenstein creates a monster. While Frankenstein's methods are never revealed, it's hinted that he uses electricity from a lightning storm to bring the beast to life.

The story was inspired by real science. Over 30 years before Shelley wrote her novel, a scientist called Luigi Galvani tried to prove that electricity caused movement in the body. His way of doing this was a little gruesome.

Galvani connected metal rods to a dead frog and put the frog outside during a lightning storm. When lightning struck the spikes, the electricity caused the muscles in the frog's legs to move, proving Galvani was right.

His idea didn't just inspire Mary Shelley's book. It also helped scientists to understand the brain's electrical impulses.

43

MARVELOUS MESSENGERS

HOW NEURONS BRING IDEAS TO LIFE

Your cells all have different jobs. Skin cells are tough and protect your body. Blood cells carry the fuel you need to stay alive. Brain cells are called *neurons*, and tangle together into chains to pass information from one neuron to another.

NEURON TO NEURON

Have you ever tried to look something up online but had no Wi-Fi? Your computer needs to be able to receive the information you're looking for, and your brain is the same.

This diagram shows what one neuron looks like. The spiky branches are called *dendrites*. They receive impulses or signals from other neurons and get ready to pass them on.

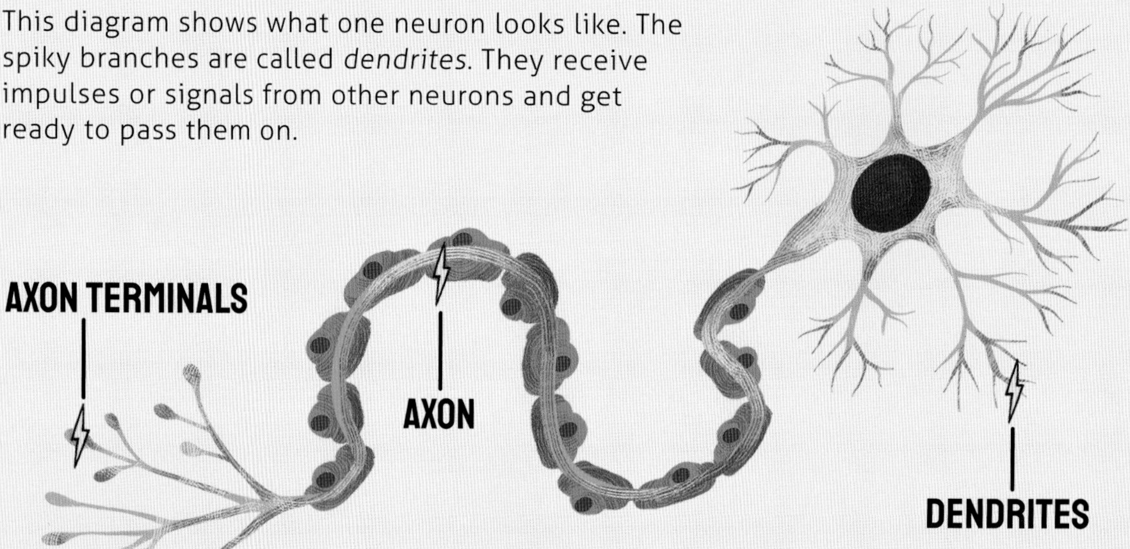

AXON TERMINALS

AXON

DENDRITES

Once an impulse has been received, it travels down the *axon* to the *axon terminals*. These terminals pass the impulse to the dendrites of another neuron, and the chain continues. This all happens faster than the blink of an eye.

PASS THE IDEA

You can re-create what neurons do by playing a game of hot potato. However, instead of passing the potato in the hope that when the music stops you don't have the potato, the aim is to pass it as quickly as you can. This is how your impulses move from one neuron to the next.

TRY IT AT HOME: A GAME OF SPEED

Look in a mirror and smile. Now frown. Now wiggle your fingers. How much time passed between thinking about doing those things and the moment when they happened? No time at all, right? That's how fast your neurons are. In fact, your brain cells can send up to 50 different commands every second.

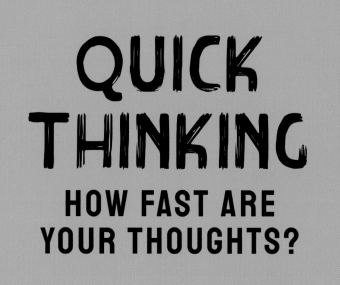

PLUMMETING
PEREGRINE FALCON
242 MPH

YOUR THOUGHTS
268 MPH

QUICK THINKING

HOW FAST ARE YOUR THOUGHTS?

BERTIE,
THE FASTEST
TORTOISE EVER
0.6 MPH

THE AVERAGE
PERSON TAKING
A WALK
3 MPH

FORMULA ONE CAR

231 MPH

CHEETAH

61 MPH

The signals from your brain need to be able to travel quickly. If they couldn't, you'd never be able to catch a ball or pull your hand away from a hot surface.

But just how fast are they? **FAST**. Signals journeying through your spinal cord can reach a top speed of 268 miles per hour (mph).

Not all of your brain's signals move at the same speed. Slower ones only travel at around 3.7 mph. If you were a mile tall you'd notice these differences . . . but thankfully you're not!

Your thoughts are faster than all the things shown on this running track.

USAIN BOLT,
THE FASTEST
HUMAN EVER
27 MPH

THE NEURAL NETWORK

WHY PRACTICE MAKES PERFECT

If a path gets walked on a lot, it becomes easier to use.
If it doesn't get used, it becomes overgrown. In many ways,
pathways leading to and from your brain are the same.

USE IT OR LOSE IT

Impulses and signals are passed through your body along
chains of neurons called *neural pathways*. The more you
use a pathway, the stronger it becomes. So, if you do
something a lot, you can get so good at it that you
can do it almost without thinking.

You've probably experienced how hard it is to do
something that you haven't done in a long time. If
you're a skateboarder, you'd find it harder to pull
off your best moves if you didn't use your board
for a few months. That's because you haven't been
using the neural pathway linked to those skills.

WHY YOU'LL NEVER FORGET HOW TO RIDE A BIKE

If you don't ride your bike for a long time, you might feel out of practice. However, you'll always remember how to stay up on two wheels. You won't even have to think about it. That's because of your neural pathways.

When you're learning how to ride a bike, every movement you make is stored in your short-term memory, so it can feel tricky to keep track of everything. However, once you've mastered it, neural pathways are established in your *procedural memory*, which is the part of your brain that remembers things longer term.

GETTING THE BEST FROM YOUR BRAIN

Eating vegetables, drinking water, exercising, and getting plenty of sleep all help to get your brain performing to its very best. Learning to play a musical instrument is also a great way of giving your neural pathways a workout.

CONTROLLING YOUR CELLS

THE NUCLEUS IN COMMAND

Imagine each brain cell is like a spaceship. The cell's nucleus would be the captain, deciding whether to fly faster, change direction, or use the lasers to fight off aliens. Each of your brain cells is a complicated machine, just like that spaceship.

PROTEIN POWER

Brain cells, like all your body's cells, have just one power source: *proteins*. Proteins are tiny particles made inside the cell's nucleus, before being sent out into the cell.

Without proteins, your brain wouldn't be able to function. The nucleus of each of your brain cells decides which parts of the cell need power for which jobs.

YOUR DNA AND YOU

The nucleus of a brain cell, like all the cells in your body, also uses proteins to build and store something called "deoxyribonucleic acid" (better known as DNA). You could think of DNA as your body's recipe. It contains all of the information about how your body should behave and develop. This ranges from things you can see, such as eye and hair color, right through to more complicated matters like how your cells work.

You have a lot of DNA in your body. One tiny nucleus alone has around 6 feet (1.8 meters) of DNA tightly packed into it. That's around the same height as a tall grown-up, wrapped up to fit inside your body trillions of times!

SAME BUT DIFFERENT

Your DNA is 99.9% identical to the DNA of every other human. That means it's just 0.1% of your DNA that makes you different.

YOUR DNA IS . . .

99% THE SAME AS A CHIMPANZEE

90% THE SAME AS A CAT

60% THE SAME AS A BANANA

JUST YOUR IMAGINATION?

THE SCIENCE OF FANTASY

Imagination is the brain's ability to picture things that aren't there. It's as easy to imagine simple things, such as your shirt being a different color, as it is to imagine something amazing, such as a *T. rex* knocking on your door. But why do you need imagination at all?

A MAMMOTH TASK

The need for an imagination probably comes from back in the days when people lived in caves and had to hunt to survive. If you're trying to catch a woolly mammoth and you fail, then it's useful to be able to imagine a different way to get it. Similarly, if you can imagine that a bear might be hiding in a cave, you're more likely to check the cave for danger, which in turn keeps you safer and alive.

Over time, humans have used their imaginations for everything from writing great books to inventing the tastiest meals. Imagination is important in science, too. If a scientist wants to prove something, they have to be able to imagine it first.

SEEING FACES

Have you ever imagined you could see a face in a cloud or a pattern? That's called *pareidolia*. It was important for early humans to be able to tell if something was dangerous or not, so our brains evolved the ability to see faces and quickly tell if they were friendly. One side effect of this is that we often see faces in things that don't have faces at all.

DID YOU KNOW?

In 1976, scientists looking at images of Mars were shocked to see a face staring back at them. However, it was just their imaginations. They weren't seeing a Martian, but a rock formation. This is a great example of pareidolia.

MIRROR, MIRROR

Your imagination can even help you to be a better friend. Some of your neurons act in the same way whether you're doing something or you're watching someone else do something. They're called *mirror neurons*, and they help you to understand and get along with other people. Mirror neurons are thought to be the reason you might wince when you see someone hurt themselves, or you suddenly need to yawn when you see someone else YAWNING.

IN YOUR DREAMS
THE SCIENCE OF SLEEP

What are dreams for? One popular theory is that dreaming helps you to store memories. When you're dreaming, your brain is filing away all the essential things and getting rid of the less important bits.

SLEEP ON IT

While you're asleep and dreaming, your brain uses what you've learned in the day to rewire your neural pathways. So your brain literally changes to help you to remember new information. This is called *brain plasticity*, and it's why it can be harder to remember things when you haven't slept.

DID YOU KNOW?
The world record for staying awake is 264 hours. That's 11 whole days and nights! It was set by American teenager Randy Gardner in 1964. He said that during the experiment he found it harder and harder to remember things or even find the right words when he was speaking. When he finally fell asleep, he slept for 14 hours and was totally fine afterward.

SWITCHING OFF

When you sleep, your brain doesn't stay in a constant "sleep mode" like a laptop or TV does. Instead, it switches between different types of sleep, such as:

SLOW-WAVE SLEEP (SWS)

SWS is deep sleep. Your brain slows down its activity, your muscles relax and you breathe deeply and slowly. Most of your sleep is this kind.

RAPID EYE MOVEMENT (REM)

REM is when you dream. Your eyes move quickly underneath your eyelids and most of your muscles stop completely so that you are as still as a statue.

If your brain doesn't move smoothly between different types of sleep, it can lead to some unusual things happening to your body, such as *sleepwalking* and *sleep paralysis*.

SLEEPWALKING

If your brain tries to wake up straight from REM sleep, your muscles can unlock while you're still dreaming. This can cause your body to try to match what's happening in your dreams—which is why sleepwalking occurs. Some sleepwalkers have found themselves cooking, ironing, and even driving while asleep!

SLEEP PARALYSIS

Sleep paralysis is the opposite of sleepwalking. You start to wake up, but your muscles are still locked in REM mode, so you can't move. Your brain is still trying to dream, so can conjure up all sorts of reasons why you're paralyzed. A common one is that a monster is sitting on top of you and not letting you move!

LOOK INTO MY EYES

THE SCIENCE OF HYPNOSIS

When you think of *hypnosis*, you probably imagine someone being hypnotized to cluck like a chicken or conquer their fear of spiders. But what is hypnosis, and what's going on inside a hypnotized person's brain?

AND RELAX . . .

Hypnotism is less complicated than you might think. It's mainly about relaxing your mind and body so that you are able to concentrate and focus. Have you ever been so engrossed in a book, TV show, or video game that you haven't heard what people have said to you or noticed how much time has passed? Then you've been in a *hypnotic state*.

WHAT IS HYPNOSIS?

When a person is under hypnosis, they become so focused on a task that they stop thinking about other things. That makes them a lot less likely to be worried or embarrassed.

When your brain is super-focused, it is more open to suggestion. So a hypnotist could get you to focus on remembering something from a long time ago, or fighting that fear of spiders.

While all brains can be put into the relaxed state of hypnosis, not everybody can be hypnotized to perform on stage by a magician. That's simply because not everybody wants to be. So don't worry—it's not possible to be hypnotized into doing something you don't want to do.

ANIMAL BRAINS

Animal brains come in all shapes and sizes. Some animals have more than one brain, while others have no brain at all. From the creatures of today to the extinct beasts of the past, there's something to be learned from each and every brain.

By studying the brains of animals, neuroscientists can learn how different parts of the brain perform different tasks, and discover how non-human brains work.

Welcome to the weird and wonderful world of animal brains.

SIZING UP
BIG MAMMALS WITH BIG BRAINS

The biggest animal brains belong to mammals. But which mammals have the biggest and smallest brains of them all?

BIGGEST BRAIN

The sperm whale might not be the biggest animal in the world (that honor belongs to the blue whale), but it does have the biggest brain. The sperm whale can grow to about 16 feet (19 meters), which is a little longer than a bowling lane. Its brain weighs about the same as two pet cats, which is more than six times heavier than an adult human brain.

BIGGEST BRAIN ON LAND

The biggest land mammal is the African elephant. Its brain weighs roughly the same as a large pumpkin. Elephants are among the few animals whose brains are at the back of their heads. It's much more common for animals' brains to be at the front of their heads.

SMALLEST BRAIN

The smallest mammal brain belongs to the smallest mammal, the Etruscan shrew. The shrew is only around 1½ inches (4 centimeters) long, with a brain the size of two grains of rice.

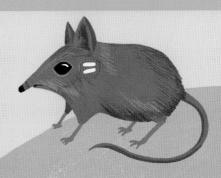

This shrew is actual size!

IS A BIG BRAIN A CLEVER BRAIN?

A big brain doesn't make an animal brainy. A sperm whale's brain is six times bigger than a human's, but it doesn't mean the whale is six times smarter. The whale needs its big brain to control its enormous body and all its functions.

For a better idea of how smart an animal is, scientists need to compare its brain size to the size of its body.

MAMMAL BRAINS
How much do they weigh?

Sperm whale	19.8 lb
Blue whale	13.2 lb
African elephant	11.9 lb
Bottlenose dolphin	3.5 lb
Human	2.9 lb
Hippopotamus	1.3 lb
Beagle	0.2 lb
Cat	0.06 lb
Hamster	0.003 lb
Etruscan shrew	0.0001 lb

CLEVER CREATURES
THE SMARTEST ANIMALS AROUND

These clever critters have serious brainpower
and they use it for some interesting things.

SUPER DOLPHINS

It can be so dark underwater that a dolphin has to rely on sound to find
its way around. But instead of having huge ears, it has a space in front
of its brain called a *melon*. The dolphin makes clicking noises
and the echoes of these noises are turned by the
melon into a map that the dolphin's brain
can understand. This ability
is called *echolocation*.

CLEVER CROWS

It's not just humans who use tools. Some
animals have been known to use them,
too. Some crows have worked out that if
they leave nuts on busy roads, passing
cars will break them open. These clever
birds have even been known to use
pedestrian crossings to safely reach
their cracked snacks.

GORILLA GABBLE

Apes can't speak like humans can, but they can communicate. Koko was a captive female gorilla who was taught simple sign language by a scientist named Francine Patterson.

Koko's brain enabled her to learn how to sign over 1,000 words. She could have conversations and even tell lies. Once, she broke a sink and blamed it on her pet kitten.

Can you work out what the gestures in these pictures mean? The emojis should help.

CHATTING CHIMPS?

Apes don't just use signs and gestures taught to them by humans. They have their own "language" with which they communicate in the wild. A scientist named Jane Goodall realized that chimpanzees have around 60 different gestures that they use to "talk" to each other.

Try stroking your chin, like you have an itchy beard. You've just said that you're hungry in chimpanzee!

ANCIENT BRAINS

WERE DINOSAURS SMART?

Dinosaurs came in all different shapes and sizes, and so did their brains. From studying the fossils of their skulls, scientists know that some dinosaurs were pretty smart, while others were not clever at all.

BRACHIOSAURUS

Most animals need intelligence to find food and protect themselves from danger. Brachiosaurs were far too big for predators to deal with, and as plant eaters they could easily find food all around them. So it was pretty easy for a *Brachiosaurus* to get by with very low intelligence. Despite their huge size, their brains were only around the size of a tennis ball.

VELOCIRAPTOR

Velociraptors are often thought of as some the cleverest dinosaurs that ever lived. However, their super-smart reputation comes more from movies than from science.

It's likely that raptors were as smart as today's birds of prey, such as hawks and eagles. That makes sense, because raptors are the great-great-great-great-great-great-great-great-grandparents of modern birds.

TYRANNOSAURUS REX

To be a good hunter, you need to be more intelligent than your prey. Therefore, a *T. rex* had to be pretty smart. Scientists think it was the *T. rex*'s intelligence, rather than its size or strength, that made it the king of the dinosaurs.

Scans have shown that the *T. rex* was one of the cleverest dinosaurs ever. In fact, it may have been as smart as a modern chimpanzee.

DID YOU KNOW?
No complete fossil of a dinosaur brain has ever been found. However, scientists can use something called a *CT scan* to build a 3D model of the space inside a dinosaur's fossilized skull and work out the size of the brain it contained.

UNUSUAL BRAINS

NOT ALL BRAINS LOOK THE SAME

Most animals with backbones have very similar brains. However, 97% of the world's animals don't have backbones, and their brains can be very different indeed. Here are two examples.

Spider
brain

JUMPING SPIDER

Imagine having a brain so big it can't fit into your head, so it has to spread out into your shoulders. Jumping spiders have brains that are about the size of poppy seeds, but with small points that spread out to the tops of their legs.

OCTOPUS

Octopuses are very intelligent creatures. Their brains enable them to solve puzzles, recognize faces, and even change color for camouflage. If a predator bites an octopus's arm off, the arm can move around on its own for up to an hour. It can do that because its brain spreads out across its body and into all eight of its arms.

DID YOU KNOW?
An octopus is an *invertebrate*, which is an animal with no backbone. Animals with backbones are called *vertebrates*.

Octopus brain

TRY IT AT HOME: TEST YOUR OCTOPUS INTELLIGENCE

Can you control your body like an octopus can? Try rubbing your belly with one hand, patting your head with another, rotating one leg in the opposite direction to which you're rubbing your tummy, and saying the alphabet backward. If you can do all that without falling over then you have an octopus's body control.

BRAINLESS BEASTS

LIFE WITHOUT BRAINS

Brains are handy for finding food, moving around, and dodging danger—but there are some creatures that don't have brains at all. Here are just a few of them.

JELLYFISH

Instead of a brain, a jellyfish has a thin layer of nerves going through its body called a *nerve net*. These nerves can tell the jellyfish when tiny bits of food get caught up in its tentacles. So it doesn't even have to hunt—it can just drift along and collect food.

EARTHWORM

Have you ever flinched when your hand has accidentally touched something hot? You were reacting to the heat. This is how earthworms make all their decisions. They have a very basic version of a brain called *cerebral ganglia*, which controls how they react to their surroundings. Earthworms are able to respond to things such as light, touch, and vibration, but they can't think about things in the way that humans do.

SEA SPONGE

A sea sponge could easily be mistaken for a plant, but it's actually an animal. It sits, stuck to a rock, and simply sucks food out of the water flowing through it. Not only does a sea sponge not have a brain, it doesn't have a nervous system at all. Scientists think that the sea sponge once had a nervous system, but got rid of it over millions of years. This is probably because a nervous system requires a lot of energy, and the sea sponge can survive perfectly well without one.

TOO SMALL FOR BRAINS

THE WEIRD WORLD OF SINGLE-CELLED ORGANISMS

Cells are the incredibly small building blocks that make up every part of your body. The average person is formed from over 37 trillion cells, but some tiny living things are made up of only one. These are called *single-celled organisms*. A single-celled organism can't have a brain or a nervous system, because just one single brain cell would be the organism's entire body.

ONE-CELLED WONDER

This single-celled organism is called an *amoeba* (pronounced "ah-mee-bah"). Even though an amoeba is too small for a brain, it still has brain-like behavior. The amoeba has tiny sensors that can respond to touch and light, and even tell it if there is food nearby.

Sensors

SLIME TIME

This page is covered in mold, but not the kind of mold you might find on an old forgotten sandwich. This is *slime mold*.

Slime mold is a single-celled organism that links up with others just like it, to become an enormous, creeping blob.

Slime mold is also surprisingly clever. It can even solve puzzles.

At the Paris Zoological Park in France there's a slime mold called the "Blob," which can find the shortest route through a maze to reach food. The Blob not only locates the correct path, but remembers the route for next time, even though it doesn't have a brain.

Slime molds aren't just clever students—they are great teachers, too. Scientists have found that if they leave a tiny piece of slime mold in a maze, then add a second piece into the maze, the two will stick together and immediately know where to go. That's a bit like gluing yourself to a math teacher and suddenly knowing the answers to your homework!

ARE THESE BRAINS?

Only animals have brains (and even then, not all of them do). But there are lots of things in the world that behave in a similar way to a brain. They keep a "body" going, take information from their surroundings, and send out commands.

Some of this brain-like behavior can be seen in human-made, artificial brains, while others are living things that appear in the natural world, such as plants. This chapter explores them and asks the question, when is a brain not a brain?

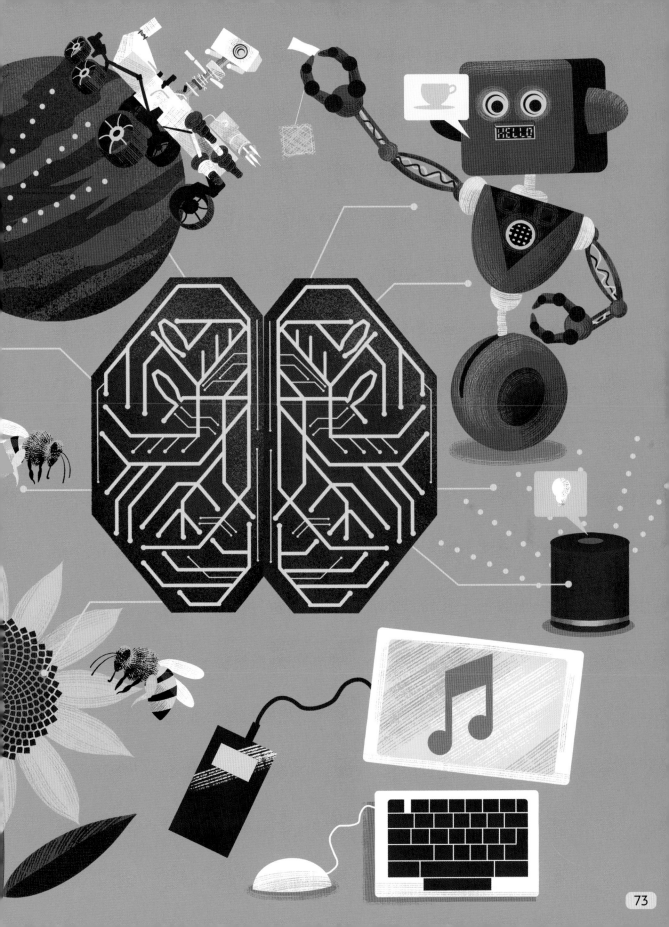

REMARKABLE ROBOTS
IS AN ARTIFICIAL BRAIN STILL A BRAIN?

A robot is a machine that can perform tasks automatically. As technology has become more advanced, the tasks have become more complicated. Some modern robots even have sensors that let them see or hear their surroundings. They can use that information to make decisions about what they are going to do next—very much like how a human uses their brain. So, does a robot have a brain?

THE BIRTH OF BOTS

The earliest robots were called *automatons*. They were normally created to do just one job automatically. For example, when Richard II became king of England in 1377, a mechanical angel was made to descend from above and place a crown on his head.

Robots have come a long way since then, but most still need to be controlled by humans. Advanced robots used in factories, for example, may seem like they're doing a lot for themselves, but they're still following instructions written by a human programmer.

THE ROBOT ON MARS

Curiosity rover is a robot that has been sent all the way to Mars. It would take a while for the rover to send any problems back to Earth and wait for a reply, so it has to be able to make some decisions on its own. Using artificial intelligence (AI), the rover can consider what is going on around it and work out where to go and what to do.

DRIVE TIME

The Curiosity rover is able to drive itself around on Mars, but what about down here on Earth? Self-driving cars that use cameras and light detection are being developed to do the things that a car driven by a human can do. It won't be long before they start appearing on roads.

DID YOU KNOW?
In 1770, a robot was built that was thought to be able to do something very clever indeed. The Mechanical Turk, as it was known, could beat people at chess. Sounds great, except for one thing: it turned out there was a skilled chess player hiding inside!

COMPUTERS v. BRAINS

WHICH ONE IS BETTER?

Your brain can handle loads of information very quickly, and each neuron of the brain behaves like a tiny computer on its own. So, could a computer ever be created that functions exactly like a brain?

POWER UP

Summit can send and receive 200 billion instructions a second, making it one of the world's most powerful computers. It's the size of two tennis courts and uses the same amount of electricity as 10,000 houses. A human brain is five times faster, much smaller, and only needs the amount of electricity required to power one little light bulb.

If you had a computer hard drive with the same capacity as your brain, it would be able to hold 18,500 movies, 150 million songs, or a book with over six billion pages.

CAN A COMPUTER EVER BE BETTER THAN A HUMAN BRAIN?

There are some things computers can do better than human brains. One of them is running lots of math calculations at the same time. Imagine trying to do several sums at once, or counting backward while saying your two times table. For your human brain, it's practically impossible.

Computers are also good at remembering long lists of information. Can you remember every website you've ever visited? Probably not—but your computer can.

MOUSE MACHINE

SpiNNaker is an enormous supercomputer that behaves like a brain—a mouse's brain. Imagine a room where the insides of 1,200 circuit boards are wired together in huge columns. That is what *SpiNNaker* looks like. However, *SpiNNaker* would still need to be around 1,000 times more complex before it could rival a human brain.

SMARTY PLANTS

CAN PLANTS THINK?

Plants are constantly reacting to what is going on around them. But how do they do that when they don't have brains?

INSIDE PLANTS

Plants don't have neurons or a nervous system, but they do have a lot of sensors. For example, your eyes have four types of *photoreceptors*, while plants have many more. This means that plants can sense light in a much more complicated way than you can. This makes sense, because light helps make food for a plant.

VEGGIE VIBES

Plants don't use their sensors in the same ways that animals use their brains. They can't think or imagine. They don't get jealous of other plants growing in better soil. And they definitely can't feel pain (so don't worry when you bite into a carrot—you won't make it cry).